AROUSING ADJECTIVES

SYNONYMS TO SPICE UP YOUR STEAMY SCENES

THESAURUS FOR ROMANCE WRITERS

LIZ ADAMS

AROUSING ADJECTIVES
SYNONYMS TO SPICE UP YOUR STEAMY SCENES
THESAURUS FOR ROMANCE WRITERS

Published by: Writer's Fun Zone Publishing

ISBN-13: 978-1-944841-72-0

CONTENTS

PRAISE FOR LIZ ADAMS' FICTION

5 stars! Oh my, Alice!

"Alice in Wonderland is truly a one of a kind book to begin with, but to be able to completely rewrite it in a very adult fashion takes talent. The author sticks true to characters Alice meets in the original books but now all encounters are very sexual in nature. Love [Alice's Salacious Adventures: Lessons From Wonderland]! Can't wait to read the next book!"

—Nic & Kenzie C.

5 stars! This book has everything

"I really enjoyed [Alice's Story of O: The Princess and the Pea]. It was so well written and it is very good. I will definitely read this book over again and recommend it!!"

—Carol Albertson-Breckenridge

5 stars! Dived in

"First time reading [Liz Adams], and wow I was sucked in. Loved [de Sade & Grimm: A Steamy Collection of Dark Delights] and I want more. I highly recommend."

—munchkinbetty

5 stars! Liz Adams does it again

"[Sherlock: The Casebook of a Salacious Sleuth] is a book with four spicy stories all relating to Sherlock Holmes. They are fun and steamy and the cases are interesting in each. If you love erotica, Liz Adams is definitely someone you should be reading."

—Taryn Schilling

INTRODUCTION TO THE THESAURUS SERIES

This is a thesaurus series I wish I had when I started writing sex scenes. While writing about a coupling, I'd spend countless hours searching for synonyms. When I wrote historical spicy scenes, I spent even more time working out if the synonyms were relevant to the time period I was writing in.

I wrote this thesaurus series for myself so that, in one trilogy of books, I can find powerful verbs and adjectives to improve my writing, plus plenty of historically accurate nouns to give my stories a flavor of authenticity.

OVERVIEW OF HOW THIS SERIES IS ORGANIZED

This thesaurus series is divided into three main sections: verbs, adjectives, and historical nouns. One book for each.

Voluptuous Verbs: The verbs are organized from early stages of desire to recovery from a sweaty bout of amorous aerobics.

Arousing Adjectives (this book): The adjectives are organized describing the body from head to toe, and all of the excitement that happens along the journey.

Naughty Nouns: The nouns are organized by date of first popular use from head to toe, then to genitals; then from foreplay to the full snog.

A NOTE ABOUT LANGUAGE: MAKE NOTE OF YOUR PREFERENCES

At first glance, many of the verbs and adjectives may seem odd or misplaced. That's where your creativity comes in. For example, instead of writing, "She accommodated his entrance," you could write, "She negotiated his entrance." In context, the reader would understand the sentence.

A NOTE ABOUT HOW THE BOOKS ARE FORMATTED

I've formatted the print edition and the digital edition a little differently due to the benefit of each format.

If you have the print version of this book, I've left space beside the words in case you want to jot down your thoughts on a particular word, i.e., which ones would be great for explicit scenes, which would be great for subtle scenes, which would be great for the meet cute, etc. You can also note your favorite words in the "Personal Favorites" section at the end of the book.

If you have the digital version, you may be able to underline or highlight your favorite terms. Optionally, others with the ebook version might see which terms you (anonymously) underlined, and you might see the terms they underlined. In this way, you can receive real-time feedback on the words readers of this ebook like the most.

A NOTE ABOUT LANGUAGE - TRIGGER WARNING

WARNING: Many of the words are profane, and some are even insulting and violent. Don't read this book if profanity and violent terminology offends you. You have been warned!

Happy word hunting!

BUT WAIT! THERE'S MORE! - BONUS PRINTABLE WORKSHEET

Go to LizAdamsAuthor.com/thesaurus to download a handsome worksheet you can use to keep notes of your favorite verbs, adjectives, and historically accurate nouns.

WHO THIS THESAURUS SERIES IS FOR AND NOT FOR

Who this series is for

The *Thesaurus for Romance Writers* series is not just for romance authors. This series is for any writer who has drafted a sex scene in their story and wants to be sure the quality of the scene matches the experience you're trying to convey.

If you want to convey a subtle, intimate connection between the characters, this book can help you find the language you need. Want to encourage the reader to experience an insatiable lust that requires hands-on reading? This thesaurus has just the words you're looking for.

Genres can include anything from spicy romance to paranormal tales, to thrillers, to sci-fi adventures, as long as there is at least one scene of sexual intimacy.

Who this series is NOT for

This thesaurus is not for writers of sweet romance nor any genre that doesn't include any sex scenes. Also, profanity and naughty words coat the pages, including words that can sound aggressive and negative. If such language may upset you, this is not the book for you.

MORE THAN JUST AN ADJECTIVES THESAURUS

This book is more than just a thesaurus of adjectives. Much more. It's an opportunity to learn while playing! How would you like to learn how to spice up your sex scenes?

At the end of this *Arousing Adjectives* thesaurus, I've added several appendices.

- Appendix A: Emotions Planner - *Recommended for Plotters Only*
  - How to make your intimate scenes advance the story and characters
- Appendix B: Writing Different Heat Levels
  - From closed doors to explicit and kinky

These appendices contain a sampling of my writing method. Have fun with them!

AROUSING ADJECTIVES: HOW TO USE THIS BOOK

If writing sex scenes is new to you, I recommend reading the "Different Heat Levels" section and practicing the "One-Handed Practice Exercises." Those sections can be found in Appendix B.

When completing the exercise, keep in mind that an "adjective" is a word or phrase naming an attribute to a noun to modify it or describe it. Readers get a better sense of how the protagonist feels when her breaths are deep, his embrace is tight, her nipples are taut, and his kiss is endless. In this exercise, feel free to overuse the adjectives.

The rest of the thesaurus can be used the same way you use any thesaurus. Whether you're in the middle of writing the scene or editing the scene, finding your favorite descriptors for the moment can be both helpful and fun.

Here's my suggested method for using the book:

1. Finish the rough draft of your story.

2. Go to a sex scene and get into the head of your point of view character. Ask yourself: What aspects of her lover surprises her, intrigues her, and excites her? His eyes? His chest? The strength or sensitivity of his thrusts?
3. Find adjectives to describe those aspects and incorporate them.
4. Now, still in the head of the point of view character, what does she notice most about herself? Her heart pumping? Her breasts tingling? Her nether regions blossoming? Her growing wetness?
5. Find the adjectives to describe her excitement.
6. Break into a pleasurable sweat, then take a moment to find release in the shower.
7. Rinse and repeat.

Use this thesaurus the way that works for you best!

Note down the adjectives you like most in the "Personal Favorites" section in the back of the paperback version or underline the words in the ebook version.

What's most important is to enjoy the process!

INTRODUCTION TO AROUSING ADJECTIVES

Generally, authors frown on using adjectives and there's a good reason. Just as adverbs can be replaced with stronger verbs ("She ran quickly" can become "She hastened"), so, too, can adjectives be replaced with stronger nouns ("She ran across the wet dirt" can become "She ran across the mud").

However, in my experience, adjectives in a sex scene can stimulate wonderful results. Notice how a mere string of adjectives — ample, budding, eager, hot, engorged, succulent, fierce, mighty, wet, stiff — can elicit delightful tingling sensations.

WHAT ARE ADJECTIVES? AND HOW CAN I MAKE THEM TEMPTING?

An adjective is a word that describes or modifies a noun, providing additional information about its: attributes, the many properties it has (hard, smooth, throbbing); and characteristics, its unique properties that makes it different from others (thick, greedy, delicious).

Overview of how Arousing Adjectives is organized

I've organized this thesaurus from head to toe, how a hungry lover might eye you—and all the excitement that happens along the way.

Note: Some adjectives are listed multiple times in different categories because they can apply to all sorts of wonderful nouns.

A word on gender language

When I describe a relationship in this book, for the purposes of clarity and convenience, the protagonist is female, and the protagonist's partner is male. These descriptions can be applied to LGBTQ+ scenes by changing the pronouns.

So, find the right adjectives to describe your nouns. An effective method is to choose a subtle and even obscure adjective. Doing so can increase the emotional response in the reader.

For example, instead of "his big member" why not try "his menacing member" or "his mythical member?"

On to the adjectives thesaurus!

AROUSING ADJECTIVES

HAIR

Hair:

- Breathtaking
- Curly
- Free
- Long
- Luscious
- Matted
- Messy
- Ragged
- Ravishing
- Reckless
- Shiny
- Short
- Shoulder-length
- Silky
- Smooth
- Straight
- Stunning
- Sweaty
- Tangled

Tasseled
Unruly
Uncombed
Voluptuous
Wild

FACE / CHEEKS

Face:

Bashful
Blushing
Burning
Charming
Cherubic
Divine
Enchanting
Fair
Flaming
Florid
Gorgeous
Handsome
Hidden
Innocent
Kind
Pretty
Ragged
Ravishing
Rigid

Rosy
Rough
Shy
Stunning
Sweaty
Sweet
Tense
Triumphant
Trusting
Vulnerable
Wistful

Cheeks:

Blushing
Glowing
Rosy
Soft
Tender

EYES / GAZE / GLANCE

Eyes:

Ablaze
Anxious
Bashful
Bedroom
Bright
Brilliant
Captivating
Caring
Closed
Dangerous
Dazzle
Desperate
Downcast
Dreamy
Eager
Electric
Enchanting
Fierce
Half-closed

Heart-stopping
Hidden
Horny
Hungry
Hypnotic
Innocent
Inviting
Jealous
Kind
Naughty
Open
Pretty
Probing
Provocative
Ravishing
Serious
Sexy
Sincere
Sleepy
Smoldering
Soft
Spellbinding
Stunning
Sweet
Thirsty
Triumphant
Trusting
Vulnerable
Wicked
Wild
Willing
Wistful

Glance:

Covert
Cursory
Fierce
Furtive
Longing
Private
Secretive
Wistful

Gaze:

Ardent
Charming
Desiring
Firm
Heavy
Icy
Incendiary
Indecent
Insidious
Inspiring
Intense
Intimate
Intoxicating
Lecherous
Lewd
Licentious
Longing
Lustful
Penetrating
Possessive
Roaming
Reckless

Relentless
Riveted
Rough
Salacious
Searing
Sexual
Shy
Steamy
Stern
Stirring
Sultry
Surreptitious
Tenacious
Tender
Unruly
Unsteady
Wandering
Wistful
Wanton
X-rated

LIPS

Lips:

Captivating
Closed
Dainty
Delicate
Dewy
Divine
Enchanting
Full
Inspiring
Inviting
Little
Locked
Luscious
Moist
Obedient
Open
Parted
Petite
Pink

Pouting
Pretty
Provocative
Quivering
Ravishing
Red
Reluctant
Rosy
Rubbery
Ruby
Satin
Sensational
Sensuous
Silky
Soft
Succulent
Sumptuous
Sweet
Tantalizing
Tender
Tense
Tight
Tiny
Titillating
Velvety
Voluptuous
Vulnerable
Willing

BREATH

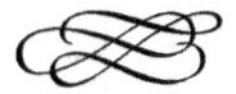

Breath:

Deep
Fast
Hard
Heavy
Lustful
Panting
Shallow
Stiff
Still
Unsteady
Wavering

PHYSICAL AROUSAL

Outer Arousal

Eyes:

Blazed with lust
Burned with need
Flickered with excitement
Gave him a once-over
Gawked
Gazed
Gleamed
Glinted
Leered
Lit up
Pupils dilated
Stared
Sparked with desire
Sparkled
Strong eye contact
Took in the sight of him

Twinkled
Widened

Mouth:

Curved into a smile
Grinned
Licked his lips
Lips parted
Pursed his lips
Smiled
Smirked
Swallowed

Voice:

Growled
Lowered his voice
Stammered
Stuttered

Gestures:

He adjusted himself
He dabbed his forehead with a handkerchief
He leaned in close
He scratched his chin
He scratched the back of his neck
He scratched his cheek/sideburns
He squirmed in his seat
Her legs slightly parted
Her skin flushed
Her toes curled

Moved closer to her
She fanned herself
She held the object close
She lifted her chin, exposing her neck
She ran her hand through her hair
She smoothed down her skirt
She thrust out her chest
She toyed with her earring
She twirled her hair
She tucked a lock of hair behind her ear
Touched her own throat

Breath:

He panted
He was breathing hard
Quickened
She took in a sharp breath

Breasts:

Heaving
Rose and fell

Penis:

A bulge / lump / bump / knob / swelling / growth / ridge / protrusion / protuberance in his pants
His member grew visibly in his pants
His pants tented
His tight pants revealed the outline of his erection

Inner arousal

Heart:

Accelerated
Hammered
Palpitating
Pang
Pounded
Raced
Skittered
Throbbed
Thumped

Chest:

Ache
Fluttered
Pain
Pang
Stir
Tingle

Blood/Pulse:

Accelerated
Heat coursed through her veins
Sizzled
Warmth flooded her chest

Breath/Mouth:

Accelerated
Breathless

Hastened
Hitched
Quickened
Salivated
Swallowed
He took her breath away
Her breath caught

Head:

Dizzy
Hair rose at the nape of her neck
Light-headed

Skin:

Flushed
Got goosebumps
Hair raised along her arms
Shiver
Tingled

Muscles:

Ached with desire
Knees weakened/wobbled

Scents:

Aroma
Fragrance
Odor
Perfume

Scent
Smell

Taste:

Flavor
Taste

KISS

Gently:

Delicate
Discreet
Gentle
Innocent
Kind
Lips joined
Loving
Modest
Reluctant
Sensuous
Shy
Sincere
Tender
Timid
Titillating

Fiercely:

Animal
Ardent
Breathtaking
Consuming
Eager
Eternal
Fierce
Firm
Frantic
Frenzied
Heavy
Hot
Hungry
Hurried
Incendiary
Lecherous
Lips locked
Love-starved
Luscious
Passionate
Penetrating
Potent
Powerful
Rough
Savage
Scorching
Searing
Steamy
Strong
Sweaty
Thirsty
Unruly
Urgent

Vigorous
Wild
Wonton
Zealous

Boldly:

Bold
Dangerous
Daring
Desperate
Determined
Eager
Ecstatic
Evocative
Heart-stopping
Hungry
Impulsive
Indiscreet
Insistent
Jaunty
Jealous
Lustful
Penetrating
Possessive
Potent
Reckless
Stirring
Tense
Triumphant
Unchained
Unlocked
Unruly
Wicked

Wild
Zealous

Exquisitely:

Divine
Dreamy
Electric
Enchanting
Ethereal
Evocative
Exquisite
Heady
Heart-stopping
Hot
Hypnotic
Incendiary
Intoxicating
Luscious
Maddening
Masterful
Practiced
Rapturous
Refreshing
Salacious
Scorching
Searing
Sensational
Sensuous
Steamy
Stirring
Tantalizing
Titillating
Triumphant

Tasty:

Musky
Spicy
Sweet
Tangy
Tart

CRY OUT

Cry:

Breathless
Ecstatic
Gentle
Helpless
Hungry
Hysterical
Long
Loud
Low
Of anguish
Piercing
Quiet
Rapturous
Salacious
Sharp
Soft
Tender
Thirsty
Thrilling

Triumphant
Tumultuous
Unchained
Unlocked
Wailing

SMILE / LAUGH

Smile:

Admirable
Bashful
Blushing
Breathtaking
Caring
Charming
Cherubic
Content
Covert
Daring
Divine
Dreamy
Enchanting
Erotic
Ethereal
Evocative
Exquisite
Familiar

Dangerous
Dazzling
Discreet
Handsome
Hot
Hypnotic
Icy
Impish
Indecent
Indiscreet
Infinitesimal
Innocent
Intimate
Intoxicating
Kind
Lewd
Licentious
Lovely
Luscious
Lustful
Modest
Naughty
Penetrating
Perilous
Pervasive
Possessive
Private
Provocative
Rare
Refreshing
Saucy
Savage
Scorching

Secretive
Sensational
Sexual
Sexy
Shy
Sincere
Sleepy
Steamy
Stirring
Stunning
Succulent
Sumptuous
Surreptitious
Tantalizing
Tender
Tense
Thirsty
Tight
Titillating
Triumphant
Trusting
Voluptuous
Vulnerable
Wicked
Wild
X-rated

Laugh:

Earthy
Erotic
Gravelly
Heart-stopping

Horny
Husky
Hysterical
Impish
Indecent
Insidious
Lecherous
Lewd
Licentious
Lovely
Luscious
Lustful
Naughty
Penetrating
Provocative
Rowdy
Salacious
Saucy
Savage
Scorching
Sensuous
Sexual
Sexy
Shady
Spicy
Stirring
Sultry
Tantalizing
Tender
Tense
Throaty
Titillating
Triumphant
Tumultuous

Unlocked
Unsteady
Vivacious
Wanton
Wicked
Wild

SCENT / TASTE

Scent:

Breathtaking
Consuming
Dangerous
Discreet
Divine
Dreamy
Eager
Enchanting
Euphoric
Evident
Evocative
Exquisite
Faint
Feminine
Heady
Heart-stopping
Incendiary
Indiscreet
Intense

Intimate
Intoxicating
Inviting
Luscious
Maddening
Masculine
Musky
New
Perfumed
Pervasive
Potent
Provocative
Raging
Redolent
Sensational
Sensuous
Steamy
Stirring
Strange
Strong
Succulent
Sultry
Sweaty
Sweet
Tantalizing
Titillating
Triumphant
Unchained
Unlocked
Unruly
Urgent
Wicked
Wild
Willing

X-rated

Taste:

Decadent
Divine
Euphoric
Exquisite
Feminine
Intimate
Intoxicating
Luscious
Masculine
Musky
New
Piquant
Potent
Raging
Salty
Searing
Spicy
Strange
Strong
Sweaty
Sweet
Tangy
Tantalizing
Tart
Titillating

NECK

Neck:

Delicate
Delicious
Divine
Enchanting
Erotic
Inviting
Long
Rosy
Sexy
Slender
Succulent
Tantalizing
Tender
Tense
Tight
Titillating
Vulnerable

BODY / BODY SHAPE

Body / Body Shape:

Ample
Big
Blissful
Blossoming
Blushing
Budding
Buff
Bulging
Breathtaking
Burgeoning
Burly (big and strong)
Bursting
Corpulent
Divine
Dreamy
Eager
Ecstatic
Electrified
Enchanting

Engorged
Enormous
Erect
Excited
Exquisite
Fervid
Fierce
Firm
Fleshy
Formidable
Full
Full-figured
Giant
Gigantic
Glistening
Glorious
Gorgeous
Growing
Hairy
Handsome
Hard
Heart-stopping
Hearty
Heavy
Heavy-set
Hot
Huge
Hypnotic
Immense
Intoxicating
Iron
Juicy
Large
Limp

Lithe
Lubricated
Luscious
Lustful
Majestic
Massive
Mighty
Monstrous
Muscular
Mythical
Obedient
Oiled
Plump
Pulsating
Ragged
Ravishing
Recumbent (reclining)
Rigid
Rising
Robust
Rock-hard
Rosy
Satin
Sensational
Sensuous
Sexual
Sexy
Shapely
Slender
Slim
Smooth
Soft
Spellbinding
Sprouting

Steamy
Stiff
Stiffening
Stirring
Stout
Stunning
Succulent
Sumptuous
Sweaty
Swelling
Swollen
Tall
Tantalizing
Taut
Tense
Thick
Thin
Throbbing
Thundering
Titillating
Twitching
Urgent
Velvety
Vigorous
Virile
Voluptuous
Vulnerable
Warm
Wild
Willing
Wistful

BREASTS / NIPPLES

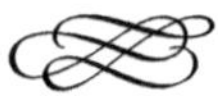

Breasts:

Alabaster
Ample
Black
Blushing
Bronze
Budding
Dainty
Divine
Enchanting
Firm
Full
Glorious
Hidden
Hypnotic
Immense
Inviting
Jaunty
Large
Little

Luscious
Modest
Mythical
Petite
Pliant
Plump
Quivering
Shapely
Smooth
Soft
Squeezable
Strawberry-tipped
Stunning
Succulent
Sumptuous
Sweaty
Swell of her
Tan
Tantalizing
Tender
Tiny
Titillating
Voluptuous
White

Nipples:

Awakened
Budding
Ecstatic
Electrified
Evident
Excited
Engorged

Firm
Hard
Inviting
Luscious
Pink
Pluckable
Plump
Red
Rigid
Rock-hard
Rosy
Rubbery
Ruby
Stiff
Strawberry
Succulent
Swollen
Tantalizing
Taut
Titillating
Urgent
Willing
Wistful

HANDS / TOUCH

Hands:

Artistic
Coarse
Dainty
Delicate
Desperate
Eager
Exquisite
Fair
Feisty
Feminine
Frisky
Gentle
Greedy
Hot
Hungry
Little
Love-starved
Manly
Masterful

Nimble
Oily
Passionate
Petite
Probing
Reluctant
Restless
Roaming
Rough
Savage
Sinewy
Soft
Sweaty
Tender
Tiny
Unfamiliar
Urgent
Wandering
Wicked
Wistful
Womanly
Zealous

Touch:

Adventurous
Amorous
Animal
Anxious
Ardent
Artistic
Bashful
Blazing
Blissful

Blithe
Bold
Brave
Breathtaking
Breezy
Calm
Caring
Ceaseless
Clever
Cool
Covert
Cursory
Dangerous
Daring
Delicate
Delightful
Determined
Discreet
Divine
Ecstatic
Electric
Enchanting
Enthusiastic
Erotic
Euphoric
Familiar
Feathery
Feminine
Ferocious
Fervid
Fevered
Feverish
Fickle
Fierce

Firm
Frenetic
Frenzied
Furtive
Gentle
Greedy
Guarded
Gutsy
Heart-stopping
Heavy
Hypnotic
Icy
Impish
Imaginative
Incendiary
Indecent
Indiscreet
Innocent
Insidious
Insistent
Intimate
Intoxicating
Jealous
Languid
Lecherous
Leisurely
Licentious
Lovely
Lustful
Maddening
Manly
Mapped
Marital
Masterful

Mighty
Mindless
Naughty
New
Nimble
Obsessed
Penetrating
Perilous
Pervasive
Possessive
Powerful
Practiced
Primitive
Probing
Provocative
Raging
Rare
Reckless
Relentless
Reluctant
Resolute
Restless
Rigorous
Roaming
Rough
Rugged
Salacious
Satin
Savage
Scorching
Searing
Secretive
Sentimental
Shy

Steamy
Stirring
Strange
Strong
Subconscious
Surreptitious
Tempestuous
Tenacious
Tender
Tense
Tight
Timid
Titillating
Trusting
Unfamiliar
Unruly
Unsteady
Urgent
Vigorous
Wandering
Wanton
Wicked
Wild
Womanly
Zealous

ARMS / LIMBS

Arms:

Alabaster
Artistic
Black
Bronze
Creamy
Dainty
Delicate
Enchanting
Fair
Firm
Glorious
Hypnotic
Immense
Large
Muscular
Mythical
Sculpted
Shapely
Smooth

Soft
Succulent
Sumptuous
Sweaty
Tan

State of Limbs:

Languid
Limp
Quivering
Rubbery
Supple
Sweaty

PUBIC HAIR

Pubic Hair:

Black
Crisp
Curly
Inky
Puffy
Raven
Soft
Taut
Wiry

VAGINA / LABIA / CLIT

Vagina:

Aching
Awakening
Blazing
Compatible
Creamy
Delicate
Dewy
Ecstatic
Excitable
Fervid
Glove-like
Helpless
Hot
Hungry
Inviting
Little
Lubricated
Luscious
Moist

Narrow
Obedient
Oily
Open
Opening
Overflowing
Peach-like
Pink
Powerless
Purring
Quivering
Rosy
Satin
Scorching
Slippery
Snug
Soaking
Soft
Steamy
Succulent
Tantalizing
Tasty
Thin
Thirsty
Tight
Unlocked
Urgent
Vulnerable
Warm
Watery
Well-bedewed
Well-lubricated
Well-moistened
Wet

Willing
Wistful

Labia:

Awakening
Blossoming
Budding
Creamy
Delicate
Dewy
Engorged
Inviting
Luscious
Oily
Open
Opening
Pouting
Rosy
Rounded
Swollen
Urgent
Wet
Willing

Clit:

Awakened
Blossoming
Budding
Delicate
Electrified
Engorged
Ruby

Stiff
Swollen
Urgent
Willing

After:

Content
Clinging stream drips down thighs
Creamy
Glistening
Moistened
Painted
Purring
Quivering
Shining
Slippery
Spent
Throbbing

ENTRANCE

Entrance:

Compatible
Consuming
Delicate
Divine
Dreamy
Ecstatic
Electric
Enchanting
Exquisite
Hungry
Infinite
Intimate
Inviting
Little
Luscious
Maddening
Moist
Narrow
New

Petite
Searing
Sensational
Sensuous
Sheer
Silky
Small
Smooth
Snug
Steamy
Subject to his thrusts
Tense
Thirsty
Throbbing
Tight
Tiny
Trusting
Unlocked
Velvet(y)
Warm
Welcoming
Willing

PENIS / ERECT PENIS

Tip:

Blue
Crimson
Egg-shaped
Mushroom
Purple
Red-capped
Ruby
Ruddy

Shaft:

Fat
Full
Robust
Stocky
Stout
Substantial
Thick

Balls:

Big
Dangling
Hairy
Hanging
Huge
Juicy
Pulsating
Twitching

Before:

Dangling
Excitable
Flaccid
Fleshy
Hanging
Limp
Luscious
Satin
Smooth
Soft
Succulent
Velvet(y)
Warm

Getting Ready:

Blossoming
Budding
Bulging
Growing
Hardening

Lengthening
Rising
Sprouting
Stiffening
Stirring
Swelling
Tenting
Thickening

Ready:

Aching
Ample
Awakened
Blissful
Blushing
Burgeoning
Bursting
Distended
Divine
Dreamy
Eager
Ecstatic
Electrified
Enchanting
Enormous
Engorged
Erect
Evident
Excited
Fervid
Fierce
Firm

Formidable
Full of energy
Giant
Gigantic
Glorious
Gorgeous
Handsome
Hard
Heart-stopping
Hearty
Heavy
Hot
Huge
Immense
Inviting
Iron
Large
Lengthened
Lubricated
Luscious
Lustful
Majestic
Massive
Menacing
Mighty
Moistened
Monstrous
Mythical
Obedient
Oiled
Powerless
Rigid
Robust

Rock-hard
Rosy
Ruby
Scorching
Slender
Spellbinding
Stalwart
Stiff
Stout
Succulent
Suspended
Swollen
Tantalizing
Tasty
Taut
Throbbing
Urgent
Vigorous
Virile
Voluptuous
Vulnerable
Well-bedewed
Well-lubricated
Well-moistened
Wet
Willing
Wistful

During:

Blazing
Brutal
Burgeoning
Compatible

Cruel
Electric
Enchanting
Ferocious
Fervid
Fierce
Flaming
Hard as nails
Jaunty
Lewd
Mighty
Penetrating
Perilous
Powerful
Probing
Restless
Rough
Rugged
Searing
Stallion
Steamy
Stretching
Strong
Sturdy
Tenacious
Terrible
Unchained
Urgent

After:

Content
Glimmering
Glistening

Moistened
Shimmering
Shining
Spent
Throbbing
Triumphant

POSITION

On Knees:
Kneeling

Hands and Knees:
Doggystyle
On all fours

Lying Down:
Reclining
Recumbent
Spread eagle

Position:
Breathtaking
Divine
Dreamy
Enchanting

Exquisite
Glorious
Heart-stopping
Hot
Hypnotic
Intoxicating
Inviting
Juicy
Lewd
Powerless
Rigid
Sensational
Sensuous
Sexual
Sexy
Steamy
Succulent
Sumptuous
Vulnerable

THRUSTS

Gently:

Bashful
Calm
Dainty
Delicate
Discreet
Gentle
Infinitesimal
Languid
Leisurely
Lithe
Maddening
Modest
Penetrating
Probing
Reluctant
Shallow
Steady
Sweet
Tantalizing

- Tender
- Timid
- Titillating

Fiercely:

- With abandon
- Accelerated
- Animal
- Animated
- Blazing
- Brutal
- Burgeoning
- Burly
- Bursting
- Coarse
- Consuming
- Cruel
- Eager
- Energetic
- Fast
- Feisty
- Ferocious
- Fervid
- Fevered
- Feverish
- Fierce
- Firm
- Flaming
- Frantic
- Frenzied
- Furious
- Hard
- Headstrong

Hearty
Heavy
Hungry
Incendiary
Insidious
Jealous
Lewd
Manly
Mighty
Obsessed
Passionate
Possessive
Potent
Powerful
Primitive
Raging
Rampant
Relentless
Restless
Rigid
Rigorous
Robust
Rough
Rowdy
Rugged
Savage
Serious
Shattering
Strapping
Strong
Sturdy
Sweaty
Swift
Tempestuous

Tenacious
Terrible
Triumphant
Urgent
Vigorous
Virile
Vivacious
Wild
Wanton
Zealous

Boldly:

Animal
Balls deep
Blithe
Bold
Brave
Daring
Deep
Deliberate
Desperate
Determined
Eager
Enthusiastic
Erratic
Fervid
Fevered
Feverish
Frantic
Frenetic
Frenzied
Hungry
Hysterical

Indiscreet
Insistent
Intruding
Jaunty
Jubilant
Lustful
Mindless
Nimble
Perilous
Pervasive
Possessive
Primitive
Ragged
Raging
Rampant
Reckless
Resolute
Restless
Savage
Stormy
Stretching
Subconscious
Tempestuous
To the balls
Triumphant
Tumultuous
Unchained
Unnatural
Urgent
Vicious
Violent
Wicked
Wild
Zealous

Exquisitely:

Agile
Ardent
Blissful
Breathtaking
Capricious
Ceaseless
Constant
Consuming
Decadent
Deep
Delightful
Divine
Dreamy
Electric
Enchanting
Energetic
Euphoric
Exquisite
Fluid
Glorious
Heady
Hearty
To the hilt
Hot
Hypnotic
Imaginative
Immense
Incendiary
Infinite
Intense
Intoxicating
Irregular
Limber

Lovely
Luscious
Maddening
Masterful
New
Nimble
Novel
Passionate
Practiced
Rapturous
Refreshing
Scorching
Searing
Sensational
Sensuous
Shattering
Steamy
Strapping
Stretching
Succulent
Sultry
Talented
Tenacious
Virile

THRUSTS NEARING CLIMAX

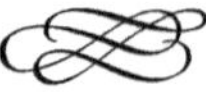

Thrusts Nearing Climax:

Accelerated
Animated
Blazing
Blithe
Bold
Breathtaking
Brutal
Burgeoning
Bursting
Ceaseless
Constant
Consuming
Daring
Decadent
Delicious
Delightful
Desperate
Divine
Dreamy

Eager
Earth-shattering
Electric
Enchanting
Erratic
Euphoric
Exquisite
Fast
Feisty
Ferocious
Fevered
Feverish
Fierce
Frenetic
Frenzied
Glorious
Hard
Heady
Hearty
Heavy
Hot
Hysterical
Immense
Incendiary
Indiscreet
Insistent
Intense
Intoxicating
Jaunty
Jubilant
Lovely
Luscious
Masterful
Mighty

Mindless
Passionate
Perilous
Pervasive
Piercing
Possessive
Potent
Powerful
Raging
Rampant
Reckless
Refreshing
Relentless
Restless
Rigid
Rigorous
Robust
Rowdy
Savage
Scorching
Searing
Sensational
Sensuous
Shattering
Shuddering
Spasmodic
Steamy
Stormy
Strong
Succulent
Sultry
Sweaty
Swift
Tempestuous

Tenacious
Triumphant
Tumultuous
Unchained
Unending
Urgent
Vicious
Vigorous
Vivacious
Wild
Wanton
Wicked
With abandon
Writhing
Zealous

SOUNDS / ONOMATOPOEIA

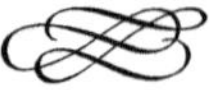

Footstep Sounds

Click
Clip clop
Clop
Crunch
Flip-flop
Plink
Plunk
Thud

Undressing Sounds

Click
Jangle
Jingle
Rustle
Shuffle
Snap
Zip

Oral Sex

Chomp
Drip
Flick
Glug
Munch
Slurp
Smack
Snort
Splish
Splosh
Squish
Trickle
Zing

Thrusts and Bumps

Bash
Boink
Bonk
Bump
Clap
Crash
Knock
Pitter patter
Rumble
Rush
Shuffle
Slap
Slosh
Splash
Splish
Splosh
Squelch

Squish
Sway
Swish
Swoosh
Thud
Thump
Thwack
Wallop
Whack
Wham
Whoosh

Growls and Moans

Argh
Croak
Giggle
Groan
Growl
Grunt
Gulp
Gurgle
Hiss
Hum
Mew
Moan
Purr
Rumble
Snarl
Sniff
Ugh
Whimper
Whisper

Cries and Yelps

Bark
Bawl
Blare
Blurt
Boom
Hiss
Hoot
Howl
Roar
Screech
Snarl
Spit
Squawk
Squeak
Whoop
Yelp
Yikes

Bed Sounds

Bang
Bam
Bump
Chirp
Clank
Clap
Clack
Clatter
Clink
Clunk
Crash
Creak
Crunch

Flop
Jangle
Ker-ching
Kerplunk
Knock
Ping
Plink
Plop
Plunk
Rattle
Rumble
Rustle
Shuffle
Squeak
Sway
Thud
Thump
Thwack
Twang

Sobs and Sniffles

Bawl
Boo-hoo
Sniff
Whimper

Afterglow

Bubble
Buzz
Crack
Crackle
Drip

Fizz
Lub-dub (heart)
Ooze
Phew
Rattle
Ring
Rumble
Shush
Sizzle
Sway
Trickle
Whirr

DISCHARGE

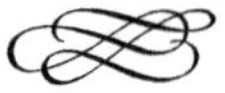

Vaginal:

Abundant
Ample
Bursting
Creamy
Divine
Eager
Infinite
Metallic
Opalescent
Overflowing
Piquant
Plentiful
Redolent
Restless
Slippery
Sweet
Sweetest
Tart

Unchained
Unlocked
Urgent
Watery

Sperm:
Abundant
Ample
Bursting
Clinging
Copious
Creamy
Divine
Ecstatic
Exquisite
Extensive
Hot
Infinite
Jerking gushes
Overflowing
Pent-up
Pearly
Plentiful
Relentless
Rich
Salty
Slippery
Sloppy
Sticky
Strong
Thick
Tickling
Trickling

A torrent of
Tumultuous
Unchained
Urgent
Volumes of
White

PHYSICAL BODY REACTIONS TO ORGASM

During:

Compressions
Contortions
Contractions
Seizure
Spasms

After:

Comfort
Consolation
Delicious exhaustion
Relaxation
Relief
Solace

After (adjectives):

Comforted
Consoled

Exhausted
Immovable
Relaxed
Relieved
Satiated
Sleepy
Spent
Tired
Wasted

BOTTOM / ANUS

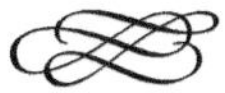

Bottom:

Alabaster
Ample
Chocolate
Creamy
Enchanting
Exposed
Firm
Fleshy
Hot
Hungry
Inviting
Jaunty
Large
Luscious
Pale
Plump
Puckered
Restless
Rosy

Shuddering
Succulent
Sumptuous
Sweet
Tan
Tantalizing
Tender
Tense
Tight
Tiny
Titillating
Trusting
Urgent
Vulnerable
White

Anus:
Aching
Awakening
Blazing
Clenched
Compatible
Dark
Delicate
Dewy
Dry
Ecstatic
Fervid
Glove-like
Helpless
Hot
Hungry
Inviting
Moist

Obedient
Oily
Open
Opening
Pink
Puckered
Quivering
Resistant
Rosy
Satin
Slippery
Snug
Soft
Steamy
Succulent
Thirsty
Tight
Unlocked
Urgent
Vulnerable
Warm
Well-bedewed
Well-moistened
Willing

LEGS

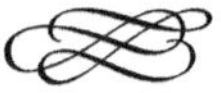

Legs:

Alabaster
Chocolate
Creamy
Dainty
Divine
Fair
Luscious
Obedient
Plump
Quivering
Sheer
Stunning
Succulent
Sultry
Sumptuous
Tan
Tangled
Tantalizing

Unstable
Unsteady
White
Wicked

FEET

Feet:

Cute
Dainty
Darling
Delicate
Delicious
Divine
Enchanting
Exquisite
Feminine
Little
Lovely
Petite
Smooth
Stunning
Succulent
Sumptuous
Sweet
Tantalizing

Tender
Tiny

SOUL / SKIN

Soul / Skin:

Angelic
Appealing
Bare
Black
Bronze
Callous
Captivating
Chocolate
Compelling
Consuming
Coquettish
Delicate
Delightful
Desperate
Divine
Dreamy
Electric
Enchanting
Erotic

Ethereal
Exposed
Exquisite
Familiar
Feminine
Fragile
Gentle
Glorious
Glowing
Gorgeous
Heavenly
Inviting
Love-starved
Lovely
Manly
Naked
Natural
Nude
Of the gods
Oily
Pale
Pliant
Proud
Quivering
Refreshing
Rough
Sacred
Satin
Sensational
Sensuous
Sexual
Sexy
Sheer
Shuddering

Shy
Silky
Smooth
Soft
Steamy
Stunning
Succulent
Sultry
Sweaty / salty
Sweet
Tender
Tense
Velvet(y)
Voluptuous
Vulnerable
Warm
Wicked
Womanly

APPENDIX A: EMOTIONS PLANNER

Contents:

INTRODUCTION

There are generally two kinds of writers: Plotters and Pantsers. As a rule of thumb, plotters outline the entire novel before writing it, and pantsers write from the seat of their pants, not knowing where the next scene will take them. Some authors are hybrids, planning a little bit before diving in with their writing. Plantsers?

In general, it is best to stay with whatever kind of writer you are. If you're a plotter and try being a pantser, you might lose track of the story and then lose interest, not knowing what scene should come next. If you're a pantser and try being a plotter, you'll find that outlining the full story has taken away the excitement of discovering where the story will take you. If you're a pantser, embrace the joy of discovering your story as you write it and avoid drafting the plot in advance until the idea of plotting appeals to you.

This Appendix A is for plotters and plantsers. So pantsers, feel free to skip this appendix and only read Appendix B.

For plotters, before writing the first scene of your book, start with determining the protagonist's goal (what she wants), motivation (why she wants it), conflict (who or what is the main obstacle stopping her from getting it), and stakes (what will she risk losing if she tries and fails to overcome the obstacles).

Knowing the character's goal, motivation, conflict, and stakes will help you know her thoughts, concerns, and emotions, creating a more compelling story. Make your story meaningful, not just sexy.

In the following sections, we'll go over what each aspect is with examples, how to include them in your stories, and exercises you can do to incorporate them.

GOAL

The character's goal is all about what she wants. In compelling stories, she'll have two goals: a long-term goal, one that takes place over the entirety of the story, and short-term goals, tasks she wants to achieve moment to moment, scene to scene.

Determine your character's long-term interior and exterior goals. In other words, what is her inner goal? What is her outer goal?

Inner goals like: learning to trust others, overcoming self-doubt, accepting love, healing from trauma, letting go of control.

Outer goals like: saving a life, finding treasure, seeking revenge, gaining status, solving a crime, acquiring new skills, winning a competition.

Once you know these two goals for your protagonist, devise a series of steps that the protagonist will need to go through to achieve her inner and outer goals.

For example, in my book *Alice's Study in Little Deaths, Aesop's Fables,* Alice's inner goal, unbeknownst to her at first, is to overcome her pride and be a better person to others. Her outer goal is to find the murderer.

Example: Outer Goal

Here's the overview of the steps Alice takes to find the murderer:

Outer Goal: Find the murderer

1. Finds clue #1
2. Finds clue #2
3. Finds clue #3, clues prove the first suspect is innocent
4. Finds clue #4
5. Finds clue #5
6. Finds clue #6, clues prove the second suspect is innocent
7. Finds clue #7
8. Finds clue #8
9. Finds clue #9, clues prove the third suspect is guilty
10. Confront the murderer

Example: Inner Goal

Here's the planning I did on what steps Alice should experience to achieve her inner goal which is to overcome her pride and be a better person to others.

Keep in mind, what I present is not the right way to write the character arc for the protagonist's inner goal. There is no right way, only your way. However, this is what works for me, and if it inspires you to try this process, have at it!

In Act 1, she starts out having too much pride. In Act 2, she recognizes that letting her pride guide her is harmful to others. In Act 3, she turns toward becoming humble and accepting humility. In Act 4, she learns to balance her humble self with a necessary dose of pride.

Once I knew her inner transformation arc in each act, I broke down the acts into lessons learned in each sex scene, numbered under each act. In this section, I don't explain how Alice comes to each realization through the sex scene. I'll share that at some later date.

Act 1: Too much pride

1. Be proud, your pride is admirable and gets good results.
2. Pride is admirable but may be a form of denial in what you can't attain.
3. It's okay to have too much pride with beneficial results, even at the cost of others.
4. Having too much pride can bite you in the ass, recognize you're too proud.

Act 2: Too much pride is harmful to others

5. Surely you're better than that person. Wait. No, you're not. Listen, don't talk.
6. Surely you're needed. Wait. No, you're not. Put your business first, what is the mission? Your feelings about yourself don't matter as much as getting the task done.
7. Surely your accomplishments entitle you to special behavior. Wait. No, they don't. Put everyone else's feelings before your own to get respect.

Act 3: Become humble and accept humility

8. Apologize to the one you offended.

9. Overcome the temptation to use pride in a situation and use something else like humility or honoring someone else. Distract yourself from your pride.
10. Someone needs help? Volunteer to help him.
11. You have nice clothes? Get rid of them.
12. You have a great body? Let people use you however they wish.

Act 4: Balance a humble nature with self-confidence

13. Feeling abused? Perhaps too much humility is not good, and a little pride is necessary.
14. Ask for help with balancing your pride with humility.
15. Allowing pride to return helps give you enough confidence to help others and yourself so everyone wins.
16. Pride is seductive but causes no ill effect in this moment.
17. Now you've returned to becoming a person with too much pride and it has hurt someone.
18. Adjust your interactions with others appropriately and learn to forgive yourself.

Each one of these inner and outer goals can be achieved in a sex scene. (They can!)

Indeed, in *Alice's Study of Little Deaths,* many of them are accomplished in sexual situations. That said, the steps can easily be accomplished in any kind of scene.

When writing your sex scene, determine which step your

protagonist needs to experience to continue her journey toward her goal. Once you know that, use the step as a guide on how the sex scene will play out.

Planning this particular story of Alice took many hours. In fact, the outline alone came out to be over 38,000 words! The book itself is over 100,000 words. But doing all that work helped me know in advance what to write to make the story meaningful, not just sexy.

MOTIVATION

We've gone over your protagonist's goal, what she wants, now let's address her motivation, why she wants it. It's fine for a character to have multiple motivations. In fact, in every scene, she'll have a specific goal and, with that, a specific motivation that is likely connected to her overall story motivation.

What's important though, in the case of her overall story motivation, is to identify both her conscious motivation (what she believes is the reason for her goal) and her subconscious motivation (what is the true reason for her goal but may not be aware).

For example, in *de Sade & Grimm: An Ambush of Cream,* the protagonist of the Middle Ages fantasy novella, Esther, has been haunted by sprays of cream on her body appearing out of nowhere. She becomes a saucy barmaid so that, when the white stripes appear, the town folk would think it was nothing more than the result of her seduction of a patron. No one would suspect her of witchcraft.

But what is her conscious motivation? For that, we need to first understand her external goal:

When Celeste de Sade, the story's detective, asks Esther why she seduces the men, Esther admits, "I know not why. When I coax a man to cram me, the cramming is delightful, but by the morrow, I feel more and more hollow inside as if I've been giving away pieces of my heart to every man I help spurt. In truth, I wish to have the same as other women. A kind husband, a family, with a home of my own and time to craft my paintings."

Now we know her external goal: to be married with children in her own house, and time to make paintings.

Based on what she says, we can infer her conscious motivation. Indeed, many come to mind. She wants to stop playing the saucy barmaid. She also wants a man who truly loves her.

For the purposes of this example, let's focus on her goal to stop playing the bawdy barmaid.

One way to uncover your character's true subconscious motivation is to repeatedly ask the question, "What would having that do for her?" (A question that comes from NLP, neurolinguistic programming, as taught at NLP Marin.)

Here's an example exercise for the story mentioned above:

What would having the opportunity to stop playing the saucy barmaid do for her?

If she stopped playing the saucy barmaid, she could focus on finding a husband.

What would having that opportunity to focus on finding a husband do for her?

If she could focus on finding a husband, she could find a man who truly loved her.

What would having a man who truly loved her do for her?

He would help her feel loved and cherished.

What would feeling loved and cherished do for her?

Feeling loved and cherished would help her feel valuable to the community.

What would feeling valuable to the community do for her?

It would make her feel her life was valuable.

What would having that feeling of having a valuable life do for her?

It would make her happy.

Let's pause here. Whenever the final line comes to achieving happiness, the exercise is done. Let's look at what she said before achieving happiness: She would feel her life was valuable. That's her true subconscious motivation.

How can she feel like her life was valuable? Does she require a man to feel valued? No. There are many ways to feel valued. Whether Esther decides to be a volunteer to the town, comforting widows or orphans, feeding the homeless and hungry, or she decides to find a man who authentically loves her and values her every day of her life, the task of fulfilling her true motivation can be done in many ways. In the meantime, while she still believes she needs a man to make her happy, I had her actions in the initial chapters of the book reflect that belief.

Good writers might use this subconscious motivation as a character transformation arc. When the protagonist uncovers her true motivation over the course of the story, then she can better know how to fulfill her true needs.

Note: When writing Romance, the reader's expectation of

the ending is for a happily ever after to occur between two loved ones. Had I resolved *de Sade & Grimm: Ambush of Cream* by having Esther spend the rest of her life happily volunteering to help widows, I would have been giving my poor readers a bait and switch. There needed to be a romantic resolution to the story based on the genre expectations.

Exercise to uncover your protagonist's core subconscious motivation: Choose one of your protagonist's overall story goals (you might want to start with an external goal). Interview your protagonist by asking over and over "What will having that do for you?"

CONFLICT

Once you know the goals and motivations of your character, consider what the conflict is. What's in the way of allowing your character to achieve her goal? The conflict can be both an inner conflict and an outer conflict.

In the movie "When Harry Met Sally," Harry inadvertently summarized the difference between inner and outer conflict by leaving a phone message with Sally. In the scene, Sally wanted him to stop calling her (goal) because she was growing fond of him and didn't want to fall in love with him (motivation), but answering the phone would mean confronting him and possibly revealing her true feelings (conflict), so she let the call go to voicemail and listened to him leave a message.

In the voice message, Harry guessed Sally wasn't answering because "(a) you're not home, (b) you're home but don't want to talk to me [inner conflict], or (c) you're home, desperately want to talk to me, but you're trapped under something heavy [outer conflict]."

An inner conflict is a challenge the character has, even though she can control it. Fears can be transformed or reframed in such a way that the character can understand them and tackle them. An outer conflict is a challenge that relies on circumstances out of her control.

The Character's Inner Conflict in the Overall Story

To determine the protagonist's inner conflict, consider what her outer goal is. What is the one aspect of herself she must change to achieve that goal?

If she must throw a dangerous ring from the top of a rickety bridge into the pits of Hell, what inner conflict would make that task extremely difficult? A fear of fire? Perhaps. A better one might be a fear of heights. Overcoming her fear of heights would be necessary to complete her quest, her goal.

In *Sherlock, the Case of the Voyeuristic Vampire,* Cynthia's outer goal is to rid the house of a mysterious vampire that roams within. Her motivation is to live with her husband without being surprised by this creature's presence. Her inner conflict is that she secretly enjoys being watched by the vampire, but to admit such a pleasure would be improper, especially to her husband.

The Character's Outer Conflict in the Overall Story

To determine the protagonist's outer conflict, consider her outer goal again. What is something out of her control that might get in the way of her outer goal?

If she needs to contact her boyfriend to tell him she was wrong to decline his wedding proposal. She's changed her mind and wants to marry him. What are all the things that might impede her goal of letting him know? Is there no phone service? Is there a fallen tree blocking the road? Is his flight set to leave in twelve minutes?

Those are all possible impediments, but they are "bad luck" conflicts, natural circumstances. There's no enemy to contend with, no one determined to make her unhappy. What might be better is if there's a person or a being that is consciously getting in her way. A deliberate antagonist.

A nearby wizard who wants her for himself will happily destroy her chances of a loving relationship with someone else. The wizard casts a spell to knock down the nearest cell phone tower, disrupting her ability to call her boyfriend. She tries driving away, but the wizard blasts a tree to fall down and block the road. She drives around the tree and the wizard casts a time bubble around her so that she moves through time slowly, hampering her from getting to the airport in time to speak with her boyfriend.

Her conflict is not bad luck anymore; her conflict has become a villain to conquer. In the crafting of the story, your possibilities open to include fighting the enemy's motivations as a possible solution, persuading him to see the error of his ways, enemies become friends, that sort of thing. The conflict has the potential to be emotional.

As an example of an outer conflict, in *Sherlock, the Case of the Voyeuristic Vampire,* Cynthia and her husband run a hotel, hoping to make a fine living from offering their hotel to wary travelers. The outer conflict is that the roaming vampire is scaring away the customers, so she and her husband must take action to rid the hotel of the vampire, a creature with a mind of his own and a lust for Cynthia to contend with.

Conflict in a Sex Scene

The way to invent a conflict for a sex scene is similar to creating conflicts for the overall story. First, notice what kind of sex scene is about to take place. Is it rough or gentle? Is it with a stranger or friend? Does it involve a nipple clamp kink she hasn't tried before? What is the setting? What are the objects, if any, involved?

Once you know these factors, interview your protagonist and ask what she believes about herself that could get in the way of having a wonderful experience. Her negative replies would be her inner conflict. For her outer conflict, ask her what external factors might get in the way of her feeling pleasure.

It's important to realize that outer conflicts in a sex scene can lead to scenes of dubious consent and non-consent because they take away the protagonist's control. However, those who choose to read stories that include dubious consent or non-consent are doing so because they choose to, it is a fantasy, and a common one at that. As a writer, though, it is your responsibility to make the reader aware if your stories include such sensitive content.

To avoid surprising the reader with potentially disturbing scenes, I recommend either focusing on keeping the conflict internal, or have the outer conflict caused by a person or incident unrelated to the couple. By having the only conflict be an inner one, the character retains her agency and ability to make her own decisions. By having the outer conflict be caused by someone other than the lovers, the intimate moments remain loving.

For example, in *Ariel's Super Power of Love,* a story of what the love life of a Wonder Woman type of person might be like, she's on a plane ready to join the mile-high club with a stranger. Her goal is to have an intimate experience, her motivation is to feel like she can be in a normal relationship, but her inner conflict is that she believes she can never be in a committed relationship. The following is a truncated excerpt to emphasize her motivation and inner conflict.

I reached into his jeans and wrapped my fist around his length. What would it be like to go out to a rock concert together? To hold hands as the music took us on a spiritual journey? Then come home, ripping each other's clothes off to celebrate the music's passion in other ways?

He granted me another taste of his lips, his tongue, his desire. He cupped my mound, a finger sliding between my folds. I moaned and gyrated. What would it be like to have this talented lover daily? Savoring me, tasting me, exploring me as though each day my body was new to him?

I embraced his head to my chest. He slipped into my entrance. Here I was with this beautiful man. It would be so easy to devote all of me to him.

I slid farther down, just enough to feel a bit more of him inside me and more of my sizzling need for him. We captured each other's eyes. My heart sank. I didn't want any other eyes in my life.

I slid down farther, letting him penetrate my core and puncture my heart. What would it be like to spend each night sharing one bedroom? To hold me in our bed. Our bed. I wanted that so much. To be able to say, "our bed."

My throat choked at the longing of saying those two little words.

I ground against him. He held me tighter, moving with me. I didn't want this moment to end. My muscles contracted. I twisted and writhed and moaned my release. I shook in his arms. Then we collapsed into our embrace.

We sat still, clutching onto each other for one minute. Two minutes. Three.

Then time didn't matter. It was just us.

He kissed me, stroked my hair, and placed a gentle hand on my cheek. "Where are you staying? We must do this again."

My throat tightened, but I was able to get the words out. "I'm sorry. I just can't."

He jerked his head back as if he had been slapped.

In this excerpt, her inner conflict of believing she must not make a commitment clashes directly with her desire to be in a loving relationship. Without the conflict, the scene would be a simple jaunt on a plane, and the plot likely would have remained intact if the scene were cut. By including the inner conflict, the reader gets to learn more about who she is.

I could have added outer conflict by having a flight attendant knock on the door and ask if everything was okay. The conflict would then be either dealing with coitus interruptus or being quiet and hoping the flight attendant would leave. Getting caught would indeed be out of Ariel's control and her lover's control. However, I wanted the focus of the scene to be on her inability to commit rather than getting caught.

Once you know the conflict your character will face, you can create a fascinating love scene. Have fun with it!

Exercise: Take a sex scene you're working on or invent a new one. Answer these questions. Where will the intimacy take place? How well does she know the lover? How rough or gentle will it be? How fast or long will it take? Does it involve any kinks she hasn't tried before? Are there any objects or devices that will be used?

Once you know the answer to these questions, uncover

the inner conflict by asking, "What might she believe about herself that could interfere with her pleasure?" (Her inner conflict.) Then ask, "What factors out of her control could interfere with her pleasure?" (Her outer conflict.)

You got this!

STAKES

High stakes are vital to making a scene great. After all, a character named Janet might have a goal of getting water from a faucet, a motivation of quenching her thirst, and a conflict of having trouble finding a cup. But that wouldn't be interesting.

If the stakes were that Janet will turn into a giant fire being that burns the house down unless she drinks a glass of water within the next seven seconds, now we have an interesting scene.

Can you imagine her tossing the contents of a cupboard in search for a cup? Perhaps she gives up and tries cupping her hands, but her hands are glowing red hot and as water splashes on her hands, it steams and evaporates. She must find a cup or bowl or container of any sort. Fast!

With high stakes, the reader is eager to find out what happens next and will turn the page to make sure Janet is okay.

(Janet is okay, by the way. She ran to the bowl of keys by the front door, flipped the bowl upside down, spilling the jangling keys to the floor, poured water into it, and gulped the water from the bowl to squelch her gut's inner fire. She survived, as did her house.)

If you're concerned that your sex scene isn't compelling enough, you can make it more exciting by upping the stakes of the scene. What might be a consequence of her actions? Better yet, what might be the consequences if she *doesn't* act?

For example, in *Alice's Snow White and the Seven Sins,* Alice is in a dream and needs to learn a lesson to wake up. In the middle of the woods, she meets a magician who offers to tell her a secret she is keeping from herself, but it requires allowing him to touch her temples to read her mind.

Her overall story goal is to use the dream as a way to learn how to avoid marrying Troy because she wants to marry her boyfriend Jack (her motivation). Perhaps the magician has the answer she seeks, but her inner conflict is that she doesn't know the magician's true intentions. The stakes are, though, that if she doesn't allow the magician to read her mind, she might not learn how to stop the wedding with Troy and might lose Jack.

In this excerpt, the magician stands behind a chair that is facing away from him.

The magician motioned to the chair in front of him.

Her head spun. Could she be the one who already knew the secret to making her love with Jack permanent?

She sat in the chair, facing away from him. He placed his fingertips at her temples.

"Relax, Alice," he whispered. His fingertips massaged her with a gentle touch. It felt good. She drooped in the chair. "Allow me into your thoughts." His voice found its way deeper inside her than just her thoughts. His fingers seemed to bury themselves into her skin, past her skull, and somewhere inside.

She felt his hands wander to her shoulders. Impossible, because the touch of his fingers stayed firm at the sides of her head. But the feeling was there. Maybe she imagined it.

He reached under her arms and clenched her breasts. She leaned back and was falling against his chest, falling, falling, making somersaults with him in the warm, blue sky. Her head spun, dizzy from the motion.

It felt so nice, spinning, head over heels, blood rushing to her budding nipples. He gripped her breasts harder. But was the grip hard enough to stay together and not spin apart?

Yes. He made sure of that when he penetrated her from behind. She clenched at the succulent breach. She needed this. Twirling, twirling, twirling. Bathing in the warm rays of the sun.

The sun set and they spun underneath a full moon, the stars streaks of light. He plunged into her, again and again, as if adjusting his position inside her, making sure they were firmly together in this tight dance.

The sun rose. The clouds puffed with exhaustion. He kissed her neck, flicked her nipples, buried his solid expression of gratitude for her beauty deeper within. It was glorious. Her heart beat a rhythm to each spin, and she released a climax of shudders and delight, clenching him, keeping him close until…

THUMP!

She opened her eyes, sitting on the chair, fully clothed, and the man removed his fingertips from her temples.

He then spoke her secret to her.

Good scenes require the character to have to make tough decisions. At any time, Alice could have left. However, in this case, leaving would have cost her the secret she needed to know that would later help her resolve her dilemma in the story.

Typically, in sex scenes, the tough decision is made at the beginning, often with the question, "Should I go all the way with him, or not?"

Your turn. What can you change in your scene to make the scene more compelling?

Exercise: The List of Twenty is a good method to capture high stakes. Choose a scene you're working on or come up with a new scene. On a piece of paper or on a digital document, number the page from one to twenty. Set a timer for five minutes. The timer is to help you escape any over-analysis and writers block you might feel. On the page, brainstorm as many possible dangers or consequences your character might face in the scene. As you write your list, invent stakes more dangerous than the ones you previously listed. If the timer beeps before you complete your list, keep going. See if you can fill all twenty lines. At the end, put a star next to the top three dangers you think would be good stakes for your character. You can use one of the stakes in the scene and, perhaps, use the others in a different scene.

APPENDIX B: WRITING DIFFERENT HEAT LEVELS

Contents

FROM CLOSED DOOR TO EXPLICIT

Closed Door Nudity - Rated G

Closed door nudity is when the reader reads all the interactions leading up to getting naked, then the scene stops, and the reader is left to imagine them stripping and lovemaking.

When to use it: Closed door nudity is used in nearly all genres that don't include any suggestive or explicit writing.

Here's an example. My apologies to those who have no interest in the billionaire-and-secretary trope.

"Ms. Lovelace," Brad said. "Please, see me in my office."

Uh, oh. Was he calling her into his office to fire her? True, it wasn't appropriate for them to have that jaunt in the conference room during last night's New Year's party, but he didn't seem to mind it at the time.

She straightened her shoulder-length auburn hair, smoothed out the ruffles in her saffron skirt, and entered the office of this year's most eligible bachelor, CEO of Peach Music Incorporated.

"Yes, Mr. Williams?"

He looked up from his computer with those piercing emerald eyes of his.

"Close the door, Ms. Lovelace."

She did.

"Lock it," he said.

Lock it? That went against the sexual harassment code of conduct, so either he was indeed going to fire her and didn't want her emotional process to be interrupted, or he had other ideas.

She locked the door.

He stepped to the blinds and closed them. Now, no one could see inside the office. Her breath staggered. She still couldn't tell if he was going to fire her.

"I have a meeting in a few minutes, and just finished lunch," he said. "Do I have anything on my lips?"

"Uh, no, Mr. Williams."

"Just to be sure..." He grabbed hold of her and kissed her with fierce passion.

Her heart pounded in her chest as if trying to get inside of his own. Her legs came loose. He had to hold her up. Mmm.

When he broke the kiss, she said, "Mr. Williams, your meeting is about to start."

"I can't help it," he said, lowering his gaze to her chest. "You look stunning naked."

She laughed. "I'm not naked."

"Let's fix that."

They did.

Closed Door Sex - Rated PG

This heat level is spicier than the previous one in that the reader gets to experience the moment the lovers get naked and respond to the beauty of each other's bodies before closing the door on the act of intimacy.

When to use it: Any books that don't show sex scenes use this approach. In spicy romance, this method can be used at the end of the story after the couple have already been intimate earlier in the book.

"Ms. Lovelace," Brad said. "Please, see me in my office."

Terrific. "Just a moment, Mr. Williams."

She yanked another tissue from the box and dried her eyes. She should have taken off work. She should have taken bereavement leave. Yes, true, it was just her cat that passed away, but the pain inside her squeezed her heart as much as if a family member had died.

She checked her compact mirror. Black splotches of mascara welled below her green eyes. Ugh. Her face was a mess. She touched up her mascara and blush, clacked the compact closed, then tucked it into her purse which hung on her chair.

She stood, straightened her hair, smoothed out the ruffles in her sundress, and braved facing the man of her dreams.

"Yes, Mr. Williams?"

He looked up from his computer with those piercing emerald eyes of his.

"Close the door, Ms. Lovelace."

She did.

"Lock it," he said.

Lock it? That went against the sexual harassment code of conduct.

She locked the door. Her head spun trying to make sense of his behavior.

"You know what has always impressed me, Ms. Lovelace? Gravity."

"Excuse me?"

He motioned for her to approach. "Come to the window."

What was this all about?

She stood at the corner window by his desk and looked down upon the traffic driving by and the miniature people walking along the street.

He positioned himself behind her and whispered in her ear.

"You see that street lamp at the street corner?"

"Yes." It looked like all the other street lamps, unlit because it was daytime and insignificant.

"That street lamp may not look like much," he breathed against her ear, "until you consider the gravity she faces."

The lamp was a "she?" Why did he give it a gender?

"I'm not sure I understand," she said softly.

"Every day, the entire planet does its best to make that lamp collapse, but no matter how much the Earth tries to bring her down, she stays standing tall, proud, and come what may, she will always demonstrate herself to be strong in the face of such challenges."

Her dear cat—gone. Her heart twisted at the loss.

"But just because she stands tall and proud," he said, "doesn't mean she can't feel the weight attempting to pull her down. I recognize that." He placed a delicate kiss upon her neck. "And I admire that."

She leaned back into him, a tear tickling down her cheek. "How much do you admire that?"

"I admire all who demonstrate such strength." His fingers

touched the nape of her neck. "For example, this zipper on your dress is feeling the pull of gravity and yet it stays at the top, wanting to give in, and go down."

He eased the zipper down, loosening her dress. Her breath hitched. Her dress pooled to the floor. Just because it wasn't the first time she stood in her bra and panties in his office didn't make it any less exciting.

He plucked open the clasp of her bra, freeing her breasts. Her heart thumped and she took in a deep breath, her chest rising and falling.

She shook off her stilettos and wiggled her toes on the shaggy rug.

He traced her shoulders with his fingertips, and the bra slid down her arms, uniting with the dress at her feet.

His lips grazed her shoulder with kisses. "I understand what you're going through." He hooked his fingers around the waist of her panties and tugged them off. "I will always be here for you."

Her chest filled with heat and aches and joy. She reached behind her, and when her fingers came in contact with the warm skin of his stomach, she found he had already unbuttoned his shirt. Farther down, she found his belt that needed unbuckling. It would be a challenge to unbuckle him without facing him.

Challenge accepted.

(End Scene)

Emotions Only Sex - Rated R

This method goes further than the previous two in that the scene shows them making love. However, the interaction focuses on the emotions between the lovers, leaving the genitals out of it. In my opinion, this is the best way to write a high-heat sex scene because the reader gets to have a clear picture of what the characters are experiencing and what they are emotionally feeling while, at the same time, not being inundated with body parts.

When to use it: This is a moment when the couple have an intimate union of their hearts, cementing their love for each other.

Let's continue the previous scenario where Mr. Williams is providing solace to Ms. Lovelace.

Her chest overflowed with heat and aches and joy. She reached behind her, and when her fingers came in contact with the warm skin of his stomach, she found he had already unbuttoned his shirt. Farther down, she found his belt that needed unbuckling. It would be a challenge to unbuckle him without facing him.

She faced him and kissed him. He embraced her. Chest on chest, skin on skin, his warmth gave her comfort while also igniting a fire within her.

She tugged his shirt off his shoulders. He released her to allow her to finish the job. His shirt, once off, settled upon her clothes on the floor.

She kneeled in front of him, unbuckled, unzipped, and unsteadied him. He tasted of intimate secrets. He moaned.

His pants and boxers were bunched at his ankles. She continued uncovering more about him with her lips.

"Not yet," he growled. He picked her up and had her sit on his solid, oak desk.

A solid desk would be necessary for the rigorous motion yet to come.

He bowed between her legs and found the source of her need. For some reason, in what she thought was his attempt to extinguish her fire, he only stoked it more.

"Brad, please," she whimpered.

He got the hint and stood, pressing himself to her.

They coupled, undulating together, communicating without speaking. Their silent words turned into dreams, their dreams into goals, their goals into plans, their plans into promises, and with a final push, their promises turned into vows. And after they caught their breath in each other's arms, they sealed their vows with a kiss.

Explicit Sex - Rated X

This steamier approach to writing sex scenes includes what is happening to every body part.

When to use it: The benefit of this scene is that it can convey the excitement between two people who are only physically attracted to each other having sex for the first time together. Since love is not a priority between these two, they can enjoy admiring all the luscious features their companion has and appreciate the great sensations they're experiencing. While the explicit nature of this method can be used in other sex scenes, writing in this manner is certainly appropriate for moments where couples explore each other's bodies for the first time.

Let's see how Mr. Williams and Ms. Lovelace first played together.

In the late evening, stars overhead, Ms. Lovelace climbed the steps toward the office building.

Behind her, a delicious, growling voice said, "I see that you, like me, are late to the party."

She turned to see who it was. Mr. Williams followed behind her in a handsome tuxedo.

"It's not midnight, yet," she laughed, lost her footing, and fell backwards.

He caught her. Wow, he was strong.

"Thanks," she said.

Was something wrong? He kept glancing at her dress.

She looked down. Oh, geez! Her breast was exposed. She fixed the dress collar and her cheeks burned.

He helped her back on her feet. Was he also blushing?

"Sorry," she said. "I don't usually wear a dress like this. My sister bought it for me a long time ago and I figured New Years Eve, why not, right? And the neckline is so deep that it would look odd wearing a bra underneath so… I'm talking too much."

He smirked with that seductive grin of his. She wanted to rip off the dress right then and there, and let Mr. Williams do whatever pleased him.

"Let's go inside," he said.

Once inside, he added, "I need to get a few things from my office."

"I do, too. From my desk." And it was true. She had left the name and number of her vet at her desk, and would need to call him to set up an appointment for her cat Brontë.

When the elevator opened, a bunch of drunk party-goers exited and even more followed Mr. Williams and her inside. Even when there was no room left, the party-goers enticed more drunk people to push themselves inside the cramped elevator. She was facing — and almost crushed against — the buttons, so she pressed the 22nd floor where she worked with Mr. Williams, and it was obvious the others wanted to go to the roof, so she hit that button, as well.

Mr. Williams stood pressed behind her and — Oh. My. God. — he had a full hard-on. With the constant jostling of the crowd, his erection lined up flush against the crevice of her ass.

"My apologies, Ms. Lovelace," he muttered.

"That's quite alright, Mr. Williams." Holy mother of orgasms, did she just tell her boss that it was alright for him to push his cock against her ass?

Her nipples budded to attention. Any harder and the elevator would also stop at floors 12 and 15.

She leaned back to get away from the button panel, but doing so caused her to press against Mr. Williams' chest.

He moved closer to her ear and whispered, "Are you sure it's alright?"

Well, the answer wasn't no, so she said, "Yes."

"Meet me in my office," he growled.

Excitement trickled from between her legs.

At her desk, she removed her panties and tucked them in her purse which she left hanging on her office chair. When she arrived at his corner office, he was sitting at his desk.

"I'm not sure what to say, Ms. Lovelace."

"You look a bit tense, Mr. Williams. Are you tense?"

"I am uncomfortable, yes."

"Let me help with that." She went to his side of the desk, swiveled his chair to face her, went down on her knees, and freed his length.

He gasped.

It wasn't as hard as before but that was easily remedied. She stroked him and sucked on his tip. He moaned.

She swirled her tongue around with slurps and sucks. He tasted of sweat and musk and man.

He leaned forward and reached down her dress. He had access to her breasts and did a magnificent job of squeezing them, clutching them, flicking her nipples. His talents made her clit stiffen. She flipped her dress high enough to get her free hand between her thighs and, oh, that slick part of her enjoyed the attention.

She stuck two fingers inside and wiggled them, stirring her arousal higher, bringing on the need for thrusts. So, she obeyed her demands and pounded her pussy with her fingers.

Mmm, yes. Her wetness overflowed out of her and onto the rug.

She chuckled around Mr. Williams' cock. How long would he be able to smell her intimate aroma coming from the rug? A day? A week?

He tweaked her nipples and she gasped. She lunged forward, taking in as much of him in her mouth as she could. Her nose reached his thick coils of hair, and she inhaled another part of his intimate areas. More musk. More man.

He surprised her by standing up. He brought her to her feet and bent her over the table. She giggled. He was cute when he was out of control.

He flipped her dress over her waist, exposing her bare bottom.

"No panties?" he said. "Damn, that's hot."

He squeezed her ass, a cheek in each hand. He clutched hard as if trying to drain a sponge. In a way it was working, because her essence came out, trickling down her thigh.

He kicked her feet apart, opening her up, then guided himself into her. She pounded the table.

"Yes," she cried. "Yes!"

Once he was fully buried inside her, he paused. It gave her time to accommodate to his girth.

Then he started slow movements, pushing in and out. That would have been delicious enough, he was successfully helping her climb a stairway to jubilation, but then his strokes got faster.

Outside, shouts of a countdown from 10 filled the air. The New Year was coming. 10... 9... 8...

Mr. Williams' formidable member thrust into her sopping pussy with such force, the desk started moving. Now he was helping her jog up those stairs of ecstasy. Her rock-hard nipples attested to it. Her dripping pussy attested to it.

6... 5... 4...

He rammed into her, and together they were running up that stairway, higher and higher and higher.

3... 2... 1...

She cried out her orgasm, clenching around his cock.

The outdoor crowd cheered.

Jets of his essence sprayed inside her. Clenching her eyes shut, she saw more colors than a fireworks display.

He grunted and jerked with his rod firmly embedded inside her, shooting his seed all over her womb. Her legs shook. Together, they reached the top of the stairs and soared away.

BEYOND EXPLICIT - KINKY AND/OR TABOO

In many blogs and erotica reviews, the highest level of heat, beyond explicit descriptive writing, is when it contains kink or taboo subjects. I'm not sure why taboo subjects are considered spicier than explicit sex scenes, but that's what I've noticed. Instead of writing an example, since such scenes can be triggering and upsetting to some readers, I'll simply list the topics. Neither list is complete, so for a more comprehensive list, I recommend doing a web search.

Kinks and Fetishes:

- BDSM (Bondage and Discipline, Dominance and Submission, Sadism and Masochism)
- Hosiery
- Foot fetish
- Voyeurism and Exhibitionism
- Role play
- Urophilia (Pee)
- Humiliation

- Cuckolding
- Age play
- Edging
- Spanking
- Gags
- Autoplushophilia (Furries)

Taboo:

Subjects Some Sites Allow:

Incest
Dubious Consent
Animal Sex

Subjects Almost No Sites Allow:

Non-Consent
Pedophilia

ONE-HANDED PRACTICE EXERCISES

Time to practice!

1. **Write a Closed-Door Nudity Scene.** Have two of your characters in a will-you-respect-me-in-the-morning situation. They had sex the night before and now the Point of View (POV) character doesn't know how the other feels about last night. Does he think it was a mistake? Will she ignore him and act like it never happened? Reveal through dialogue, facial expressions, and physical movements, that the other person is pleased with what transpired the night before and wants a repeat performance. End the scene before any clothes are removed.
2. **Write a Closed-Door Sex Scene.** Continue the story using the Closed-Door Sex method, removing their clothes and ending the scene before any hanky-panky takes place. Flip through this book to use strong adjectives.
3. **Write an Emotions-Only Sex Scene.** Continue the scene, showing the two coupling, but only

reveal their emotions and avoid mentioning their body parts. Try out some of the strong adjectives in this book.

4. **Write an Explicit Sex Scene.** Now go back to writing that explicit scene of the two of them the night before when they first had sex. Go wild with the adjectives! Evaluate when the use of adjectives feels like too many. See how it feels!

YOUR PERSONAL FAVORITES

I've found that I love nearly all the adjectives. However, if you find there are ones you like more than the others, note down here which adjectives are your favorites so that you don't need to keep flipping through the pages.

AUTHOR'S NOTE

I hope this has been, and will often be, a helpful resource for you.

Having written so much erotica (20 books and counting!), I thought this *Thesaurus for Romance Writers* series would be a great venue to drip some of my favorite writing techniques. And I hope that by the end, I wasn't the only one dripping.

Please let me know if there are sections and terms you uncovered that are missing from these books so that I may update them. You can email me at LizAdams-Books@gmail.com and put THESAURUS WORDS in all-caps in the subject line so that I don't accidentally miss your email.

Also, check out the other books in this series if you want more synonym help: *Voluptuous Verbs* and *Naughty Nouns in Historical Fiction*.

And hey! I encourage you to try all the exercises and templates in this series. Every master starts a disaster. The way to master your writing is by drafting and editing and getting feedback on your writing, over and over.

The good news is that writing sex scenes is fun!

As my friend and author Chloe Adler once said in describing the process of writing erotica, "You write some, then go to bed. Write some more, then go to bed. Write some more, then go to bed." Your readers will get the benefit of reading your steamy scenes in bed without having to alternate.

For all you readers of saucy tales, if you're interested in discovering which sexy superhero you are, take my quiz at http://www.LizAdamsAuthor.com. You can also join my reader community and get a free short story about what Wonder Woman's sex life might be like!

UNLOCK THE SECRETS TO WRITING IRRESISTIBLE SEX SCENES

Discover the Perfect Words to Elevate Your Romantic Scenes

This *Thesaurus for Romance Writers* series comprises of three passionate volumes dripping to satisfy your needs, each designed to elevate your writing and make your love scenes steamy:

1. Voluptuous Verbs

Why settle for mundane descriptions like "she took off his pants" when you can spice things up. Replace it with, "She unbuckled, unzipped, and unsteadied him." Find verbs that penetrate your scenes and leave your readers panting. This thesaurus includes writing tips on how to use the bedroom scene to develop the heroine's inner growth, her inner and outer consequences, the relationship's consequences, the subtext of the scene, and the wild card.

2. Arousing Adjectives (this book)

While overusing adjectives in regular scenes is a faux pas, they are indispensable when the clothes come off and the lovemaking begins. Dive into words that paint vivid pictures, like "sprouting, thick, eager, hot, frenzied, throbbing, strong," for him, and "supple, taut, pluckable, quivering, tangy, velvety, wet," for her. These adjectives will transform your spicy scenes into scenes your readers will read again and again. Included in this thesaurus are exercise on how to write at different heat levels, and how to incorporate the character's goal, motivation, conflict, and stakes in your delectable, lip-smacking scenes.

3. Naughty Nouns

A perfect resource for historical romance writers! This book of synonyms is your go-to guide to determine whether grabbing hold of his "length" fits the time period of your Regency romance. Which terms did they use back then? Discover the historically accurate terms that set the mood just right. This thesaurus includes tips on how to use explicit words to incite excitement instead of sounding like an anatomical textbook.

A Must-Have Resource for Every Romance Writer

Whether you're crafting a steamy Regency romance or a contemporary love story, use the books in the *Thesaurus for Romance Writers* series — invaluable resources that will help you find the perfect words to set hearts racing and pulses pounding in your spicy scenes with captivating synonyms. It has been a game-changer for me, and I hope it will be for you too.

ACKNOWLEDGMENTS

I started the *Thesaurus for Romance Writers* series when provocative historical author and friend Regina Kammer guided me and other authors to Jonathon Green's outstanding online interactive timeline of sexy terms and their first moments of popular use. The timeline focused on historical synonyms for genitalia and intercourse.

From there, I launched into other sources, ones which provided synonyms for words not addressed by the timeline. Most of the new terms came from a standard thesaurus. Then, I added terms not originally meant to be sexy. For example, synonyms for "breaking apart into pieces" were terms I categorized under Climax.

Over the years of dedicated thesaurus usage, the list of words became longer. And, oh, much longer. After reading such historical erotica like *The Autobiography of a Flea* and *My Secret Life: An Erotic Diary of Victorian London,* and after finding a few short lists of sensual terms elsewhere, I added even more words to the mix.

Once I completed the list, I studied the layouts of other Romance Thesaurus books—including ones by Cara Bristol, Valerie Howard, and Stefanie Olsen—and determined the layout I thought was most useful.

Lastly, my brilliant writing coach Beth Barany helped me with edits and ways to market this series.

The inviting covers were designed by 100 Covers, and I appreciate all the hard work they put into the design.

And thank you, dear writer. The world needs your stories. *I* need your stories.

Keep writing!

~Liz

ABOUT THE AUTHOR

Award-winning author of best-selling spicy, paranormal fairytales, Liz Adams tires her hands at the keyboard spinning steamy, surrealistic fantasies — some historical, some contemporary, some futuristic — so that her readers can also tire out their hands until the happy endings. She loves leaving her readers breathless and soaked.

Want to know a secret? Playing loud music while reading might hide your squeals of delight. Just sayin'.

She lives in the gorgeous San Francisco Bay Area, and in her spare time, she enjoys movies on the couch cuddling with her spouse and two cats.

If you enjoyed this book, please write a review!

Liz would love to know how you heard about her ebook, so drop her a line at LizAdamsBooks@gmail.com or at her website:

http://www.LizAdamsAuthor.com.

She's always eager to connect with her readers and would love to hear from you.

MORE BOOKS BY WRITER'S FUN ZONE PUBLISHING

OVERCOME WRITER'S BLOCK: A SELF-GUIDED CREATIVE WRITING CLASS TO GET YOU WRITING AGAIN

(Writer's Fun Zone Book 1)

THE WRITER'S ADVENTURE GUIDE: 12 STAGES TO WRITING YOUR BOOK FOR NOVELISTS AND CREATIVE NONFICTION WRITERS

(Writer's Fun Zone Book 2)

TWITTER FOR AUTHORS: SOCIAL MEDIA BOOK MARKETING STRATEGIES FOR SHY WRITERS

(Writer's Fun Zone Book 3)

PLAN YOUR NOVEL LIKE A PRO: AND HAVE FUN DOING IT!

(Writer's Fun Zone Book 4)

7 ESSENTIAL KEYS TO PLANNING YOUR NOVEL: STORY PREPARATION FOR PANTSERS

(Writer's Fun Zone Book 5)

MASTERING DEEP POINT OF VIEW: SIMPLE STEPS TO MAKE YOUR STORIES IRRESISTIBLE TO YOUR READERS

by Alice Gaines

ALSO BY LIZ ADAMS

Fairy Tale Erotica

Alice's Salacious Adventures, Lessons From Wonderland

(Adventures of Alice, Book 1)

A titillating two-book collection

Alice's Story of O, Princess and the Pea

(Adventures of Alice, Book 2)

An interactive, spicy fairytale

Alice's Frisky Freaky Friday, Hansel and Gretel

(Adventures of Alice, Book 3)

A body-swapping, dark fairytale

Alice's Snow White and the Seven Sins

(Adventures of Alice, Book 4)

A reverse-harem spicy fairytale

Alice's Labor of Love, Tasting Cinderella

(Adventures of Alice, Book 5)

An intoxicating, oral fairytale

Alice's Study in Little Deaths, Aesop's Fables

(Adventures of Alice, Standalone)

A suspenseful, spicy fairytale

Goldie's Locks and the Three Men

(A Modern Erotic Fairy Tale Fantasy for Women)

What if the only way to find the right man was to instead find the right men?

Ariel's Super Power of Love

Ever wonder what Wonder Woman's love life was like?

Sherlock; The Casebook of a Salacious Sleuth

(4 Spicy Romantic Short Stories)

Feeding his carnal appetite one case at a time.

de Sade & Grimm; A Spicy Collection of Dark Delights

(4 Supernatural Short Stories)

Can you resist the pleasure when evil claims you?

The Origin of Tinkerbell

(A Modern Erotic Fairy Tale Fantasy for Women)

Time stops for the playful.

Maid Mary and Robin Hood's Merry Men

(A Dark Romance)

A mask can hide you from yourself.

What if your beloved paralyzed you and removed your mask?

Short Stories

Amy "Red" Riding's Hood

(Fairy Tale Erotica)

Would you submit to the beast within him?

Breaking Free

(A Kidnapping Romance)

When society suppresses your femininity and your kidnapper encourages it, how can you hate him?

ALINA SAID, CALL ME MAYBE

(A Short Romance)

How far would you go, letting a stranger caress you in public?

SHERLOCK; THE CASE OF THE RIPPED BODICE

(A Spicy Romantic Short Story #1)

Your client fears he may be Jack the Ripper? Terrific.

SHERLOCK; THE CASE OF THE INVISIBLE LOVER

(A Spicy Romantic Short Story #2)

Who haunts her bed?

SHERLOCK; THE CASE OF SINBAD'S SEDUCTION

(A Spicy Romantic Short Story #3)

What will you do when a night of vengeful passion leads to a perilous mystery?

SHERLOCK; THE CASE OF THE VOYEURISTIC VAMPIRE

(A Spicy Romantic Short Story #4)

His penetrating gaze awakens your desires.

DE SADE AND GRIMM; AN ENCHANTMENT OF LEAVES

(A Dark Supernatural Short Story #1)

What if an unholy fiend unleashed your darkest desires?

DE SADE AND GRIMM; A SEDUCTION OF CLAY

(A Dark Supernatural Short Story #2)

You awake. No memory. The Clay Master claims he is your husband. Will you yield?

DE SADE AND GRIMM; AN AMBUSH OF CREAM

(A Dark Supernatural Short Story #3)

How can she fight the invisible, hedonistic foe?

de Sade and Grimm; A Menace of Silk

(A Dark Supernatural Short Story #4)

What invisible force is hell-bent on claiming her?

Short Stories in Anthologies

"The Artist" in Sensexual: A Unique Anthology 2013 Vol 1

If you were a succubus and spotted his morning growth, what would you do?